W9-BNI-816

Word List

Here is a list of words that might make it easier
to read this book. You'll find them in boldface
the first time they appear in the story.

nestled	NE-suhld
forbidding	fer-BI-ding
vegetables	VEJ-tuh-buhls
veil	vayl
tunic	TOO-nik
satchel	SA-chuhl
jagged	JA-guhd
chasm	KA-zuhm
waddled	WAH-duhld
anxiously	ANK-shuhs-lee
oozed	oozd
seized	seezd

Barbie™

Rescue of the Unicorn

BARBIE and associated trademarks are owned by and used under
license from Mattel, Inc. © 1999 Mattel, Inc. All Rights Reserved.
Published by Grolier Books, a division of Grolier Enterprises, Inc.
Story by Rita Balducci. Photo crew: James Aitee, Patrick Kittel, Dave Bateman,
Susan Cracraft, Shirley Ushirogata, Mark Adams, and Lisa Collins.
Printed in the United States of America.
ISBN: 0-7172-8886-2

G

GROLIER
B O O K S

Chapter One

Barbie hurried down the dirt road, carrying a wooden bucket. She was headed toward the village well.

"Good morning, Barbie!" called a friendly voice from across the street.

Barbie turned to smile at a gray-haired man. He was loading a wagon with hay.

"Good morning, Mr. Baker!" replied Barbie pleasantly. She continued to walk quickly down the road. She didn't want to stop to chat today. She was already late.

Barbie's village was **nestled** between

two large mountains. One was called Morning Mountain. It was lush and green, and the sun shone on it all day. The villagers had built their homes facing this sunny mountain. The other was called Midnight Mountain. Bare and rocky, it was always in shadow. A thick forest surrounded Midnight Mountain, making it seem even more **forbidding.** And nobody from the village ever went to the forest. Nobody, that is, except Barbie.

When she came to a fork in the road, Barbie stopped. To the right was the way to the well. To the left was an overgrown path that disappeared into a meadow. That was the way to the forest. Barbie looked back over her shoulder. No one was nearby. Quickly she hid her water bucket in some bushes. Then she turned and swiftly made her way down the path to the left. As she ran through the tall grasses, Barbie could see the trees at the edge of the forest that lay ahead. They waved gently in the breeze. They seemed to be saying, "Come. We've been waiting."

Barbie stepped into the woods and took a deep breath. The sweet smell of pine tickled her nose. The fallen needles made the ground soft under her feet. Sunlight and shadows danced among the thick trees.

Barbie called softly, "Skylar?" She looked around but didn't see her small friend. "Are you here?" Barbie waited in silence for a moment. She listened. Was she too late?

Suddenly she felt soft feathers flutter past her cheek. Something settled on her shoulder.

"Skylar!" cried Barbie. "You startled me!"

The bluebird twittered. He had brown eyes and bright blue wings. Barbie reached into her pocket and offered the bird a piece of bread.

After taking the bread, the bird looked up and said, "Thanks." Still munching, he added, "Too bad you don't have the excellent vision of a bird. Then you would have seen me."

Barbie looked sideways at her friend and frowned. "Just like you saw that cat, smartypants?" she asked, laughing.

Barbie had saved the bird from a hungry cat. She had hardly believed her ears when the bluebird had thanked her! To repay the favor, the magical bird had promised to show her a secret of the forest.

"I'm sorry I'm late," Barbie apologized. "What secret do you have to show me today?"

"Look!" Skylar said.

Barbie heard a rustle in the bushes. Suddenly a shimmering white horse stepped out of the shadows. Then Barbie noticed a slender, spiraling horn on the animal's forehead.

Barbie gasped. "A unicorn!"

The unicorn approached Barbie without fear. Barbie gently stroked the animal's soft nose. She reached out to touch its horn.

"The unicorn wanted to meet you," Skylar

explained. "I told her all about you."

Barbie turned to Skylar and asked, "Does she speak, like you?"

Skylar shrugged. "Of course not. What do you think this is, a magic show? I'm the only talking animal around here."

The unicorn whinnied and stomped her foot.

"Okay, okay, I'll ask her!" Skylar said. He turned to Barbie. "She wants to know if you would like to have a ride." Then he added, "From her, of course. You're a little big for me."

"Could I?" Barbie said breathlessly.

In reply the unicorn knelt down on the soft pine needles. Barbie gently climbed onto the animal's back.

The magical creature nodded her head to the bird. Then she took off at a gallop. Skylar followed close behind. Although she had neither saddle nor reins, Barbie had no trouble staying on the unicorn's back. The ride was fast but smooth.

5

"I feel like I'm flying!" Barbie cried.

The bluebird laughed, "Welcome to the flock!"

Then Skylar took the lead. The bird led Barbie and the unicorn deep into the forest. Finally they 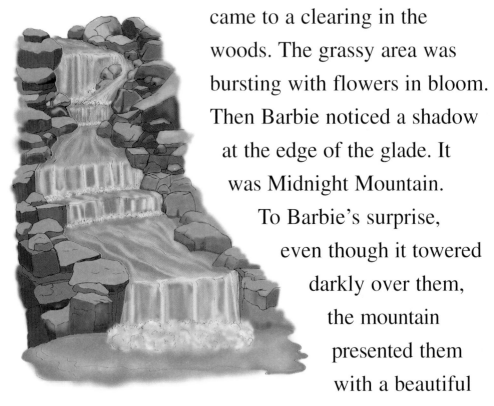 came to a clearing in the woods. The grassy area was bursting with flowers in bloom. Then Barbie noticed a shadow at the edge of the glade. It was Midnight Mountain. To Barbie's surprise, even though it towered darkly over them, the mountain presented them with a beautiful sight. A stream tumbled down its side. The sparkling water at the bottom bubbled into a large, clear pool.

"Please," Barbie called to the unicorn, "may we stop here?"

The unicorn came to a graceful stop and knelt again. Barbie hopped off. The animal walked over to the pool and began to drink.

Skylar fluttered onto Barbie's shoulder. He whispered to her, "This place is called the Enchanted Glade. It's for animals only. Humans aren't allowed. I think the rule's a little silly, though." Skylar puffed up his chest. "Besides, I've decided that you're special, Barbie."

"Thank you, Skylar," Barbie answered. "I'm sure lucky to have a friend like you!"

The unicorn trotted back over, and soon the three began to play a game of tag. They chased one another around and around the grassy area.

Afterward, Skylar took a bath while the unicorn nibbled at some grass. Barbie picked some daisies. She braided the stems together to make a necklace. The sun was beginning to set behind the mountain. Barbie wished that the afternoon didn't have to end. "I wish we could stay here forever," she sighed.

"Mmm," Skylar nodded. He was busy combing his feathers with his beak.

Suddenly the unicorn stomped and snorted.

"All right, all right," Skylar grumbled, "don't twist your horn in a knot! I'm just about finished." The wet little bird shook himself off. "We had better start heading back," he explained to Barbie. Then he noticed the strand of daisies in her lap. "What are you doing?"

"I'm making a daisy necklace," Barbie answered. "This place is so beautiful that I want to take a bit of it home with me." She tied off the ends and placed the flowers around her neck. Then she climbed onto the unicorn's back.

Soon the three friends had reached the edge of the forest. Barbie hopped off the unicorn and thanked her. The majestic beast bowed her white head. Then she disappeared into the forest.

"Oh, Skylar," Barbie said, beaming, "how

can I ever thank you?"

The funny little bird thought for a moment. Then he replied, "By bringing a picnic lunch tomorrow. Bread is fine for me, but our friend with the horn prefers **vegetables.**" The small animal twittered again and flew away.

Barbie shook her head and laughed. Then she found her bucket in the bushes and hurried to the well.

In her cottage that night, Barbie wore the daisy necklace to bed. She slept more deeply than she ever had before. She did not hear the wind begin to roar outside her window. Nor did she feel its bitter cold. As she slept, Barbie had no idea what terrible changes her one small act had caused.

Chapter Two

Barbie sat up in bed with a start. She had slept much later than usual. Even though it was morning, outside her window the sun seemed hidden by a **veil.** Barbie decided to go straight to the forest. Household chores could wait when there was a unicorn to ride!

She climbed out of bed and began to change out of her nightgown. But when she took off the flower necklace, Barbie suddenly felt the sharp coldness of the room. Shivering, she pulled on a heavy shirt and her blue **tunic.**

"That's strange," Barbie thought. "Summer

mornings are never this cold." Looking out her window, she added, "Or this dark." It looked as if a storm were brewing. But there wasn't a cloud in the sky. The wind howled outside.

Barbie shook her head. She would ask Skylar about this weird weather. He would know. She finished dressing and slipped the flower chain back over her head. Oddly enough, that seemed to make her feel warmer.

After breakfast, Barbie grabbed her brown leather **satchel.** She filled the bag with some bread, fresh raspberries, and potatoes. "I don't have time to pull carrots from the garden," she thought. "I hope the unicorn likes potatoes." Barbie looked out at the darkness again. "I'd better wear my cape today," she said, "just in case it rains." Then she grabbed a small metal lantern and several extra candles. She tied up the satchel and slung it over her shoulder. Before long, Barbie was ready to go.

That morning no one stopped Barbie to ask where she was going. No one was around. The village was dark and silent. Thunder rumbled in the distance.

"It will still be beautiful in the Enchanted Glade," Barbie thought, walking even faster. But when she reached the forest, she stopped. Everything was different. The trees waved her away as they thrashed in the wind.

"Beware! Beware!" they seemed to moan.

Barbie stepped into the forest. "Skylar?" she called. But the sound of her voice was lost in the wind and the trees. She tried again. "Skylar! Hello?"

Just then the bluebird came diving at her through the trees. "Hurry! There's no time to lose!" he screeched. "Follow me!"

Barbie had no chance to ask questions. She raced after her friend. When they rounded a corner, she tripped on a sharp rock. "Owww!" she cried, landing hard. Then she realized that the path was covered with rocks and branches. "That's funny," she thought. "Yesterday the path was carpeted with soft pine needles."

Barbie was out of breath by the time the bluebird stopped. They were in the Enchanted Glade again. But this time, what Barbie saw brought tears to her eyes.

The trees were bare and drooping. There were no birds singing. Not one flower bloomed. The waterfall now looked like an icy staircase up the mountainside. The pool was frozen into a thick sheet of ice.

"Over here," the bird called in a sad voice.

Barbie looked down at the frozen earth where Skylar stood. It was torn up by hoofprints. A net made of heavy rope lay on the ground.

"The unicorn?" Barbie guessed.

Skylar nodded. "She has been captured."

Barbie shook her head in disbelief. "But how? Why?" she asked.

"Because of what you did," replied a soft, sweet voice.

Barbie whirled around. She didn't see anyone. "Who said that?" she whispered.

"I did," the voice replied. Then Barbie noticed a tiny person, no bigger than a bird, standing on a branch. She looked like a small child dressed in a pink dress. Her small wings shimmered. There was a warm, pink glow all around her. Barbie gasped. "A fairy!"

"I am Queen of the Fairies," said the tiny creature. "The unicorn was captured because you disturbed the Enchanted Glade."

Chapter Three

Barbie couldn't believe her ears. "I don't understand," she began. She stared at the fairy in disbelief. "What could I have done to make this happen?"

The Queen of the Fairies explained, "You didn't do anything to the unicorn. I know you meant her no harm. Nothing is ever to leave the Enchanted Glade." She pointed to Barbie's flower necklace. "Not even one daisy." Then the fairy turned to Skylar and added, "That is why humans are never to be brought here."

Skylar protested, "But nobody ever told

me that part! I wouldn't have allowed her to leave with the flower necklace if I had known."

The queen just shook her head sadly.

"But what does that have to do with the unicorn?" Barbie asked. "And why is everything so cold and dark?"

The fairy flitted over to a rock. She still glowed with a rose-colored light. Barbie could not take her eyes off the tiny creature.

Then the queen explained. "A very wicked wizard lives at the top of Midnight Mountain. The beauty of the Enchanted Glade used to keep the wizard trapped there. Every flower helped protect the valley from him. But when the glade was disturbed, its power was weakened. The wizard was able to leave the mountaintop and capture the unicorn."

Skylar interrupted, "And the wizard captured her because only the unicorn's magic can restore the beauty of the Enchanted Glade?"

The queen nodded. "Exactly. Without the unicorn, the forest and everything around it will freeze from the wizard's icy spell."

"My village!" Barbie cried. "I'm so sorry." Tears welled up in her eyes as she sank to the ground. She looked sadly at the flower chain around her neck. If only she had known! Suddenly she stood up and declared, "I want to make it right. Please tell me how to fix what has been done."

"There's only one hope," the fairy queen explained. "Since you and Skylar disturbed the glade, you are the only ones who can rescue the unicorn. The wizard has her trapped in his cave at the top of Midnight Mountain."

"But what can I do against a wizard?" wondered Barbie. "I'm only a human."

"And I'm only a bird!" Skylar added.

The queen pointed again to Barbie's necklace. "Your flower chain is magical. It will protect you from the wizard's powers. But beware: he has put three obstacles in your path. You must overcome them all to free the unicorn. But you haven't much time," the queen added. "If the unicorn isn't returned to the glade by the time the sun sets today, all hope will be lost. The wizard will rule the mountains, and everything will become frozen forever!"

"I will do it!" declared Barbie.

"Good for you!" cheered the bluebird.

"And Skylar will help me!" Barbie stated.

"I will?" gulped the small bird.

Barbie turned to face the mountain, her eyes looking for a path. Skylar flew to her shoulder.

"We can do this," Barbie told her friend.

The bird looked up at the dark, **jagged** rocks of the cold mountain. "Maybe *you* can do this, but I just remembered—I have to be somewhere."

Barbie turned to look the small bird in the eye. "I thought we were a team, Skylar?"

"Okay, okay," Skylar finally agreed.

Barbie smiled at her small friend. She would be glad to have him along. Then Barbie turned back to the fairy and asked, "What are the obstacles?" But the Queen of the Fairies was gone.

Barbie sighed. "I guess we'll have to find out for ourselves."

"Oh, goodie," added the bluebird.

Barbie looked up at the sky. The sun was low over the valley. "It's still morning," she said. "But sunset will come before we know it. Let's go."

Barbie took a deep breath. Then she began to run. Skylar followed. The two raced through the glade to the base of Midnight Mountain. There they stopped. The mountain and its waterfall were surrounded by large boulders.

Barbie reached out to grasp a rock to help her climb. Suddenly she shouted in pain and fell backward.

"What happened, Barbie?" cried Skylar. "Are you all right?"

Barbie rubbed her hands. "This rock is as hot as fire," she explained. Gently she touched another rock with her fingertip. She winced. "So is this one!" Barbie soon found that all of the rocks surrounding the waterfall were burning hot. She shook her head and sat down to think.

"I guess this is the first obstacle," Skylar pointed out.

Barbie nodded and touched the magical chain around her neck. "And I guess this can't protect me from burnt hands and feet."

Suddenly Skylar had an idea. Quickly he flew up the mountain. He landed on a ledge. "Just as I thought," he said to himself. Then he flew back down to the base of the mountain. "The ground up there is cold," he told Barbie. "Too bad you can't fly over the burning rocks, like me."

Barbie closed her eyes and thought hard. "I can't climb over the hot rocks. And I certainly can't fly. I need a ladder." She looked around.

Her eyes fell on the frozen waterfall.

"Or stairs!" she cried. "Quick! Skylar! Gather as much dead grass and as many pine needles as you can."

The small bird shook his head and replied, "I don't get it, Barbie."

"You'll see," Barbie promised.

They quickly made a pile. Using her cape as a bag, Barbie stuffed it full of grass and needles. Next she filled her satchel to the brim. Then, slowly, Barbie stepped onto the ice on the pond. She tested it with one foot to see if it would support her full weight. Sure enough, the water was frozen solid.

"I hope this works," she said. Barbie carefully crossed the pond to the base of the waterfall. Then she began to sprinkle the dead grass and pine needles onto the "first step" of the slippery waterfall. She took a step up. It worked! The grass and pine needles kept her

feet from slipping. She sprinkled more over the ice and made it up another level. Step by slippery step, she climbed the icy waterfall.

Skylar flew alongside Barbie, pulling grass out of her cape and bag. He sprinkled it over the ice whenever Barbie started to slide back down. "You're almost there!" he cheered.

When Barbie reached the top of the waterfall, she sank to the ground. She'd done it!

"Hooray!" screeched Skylar, flying in circles around her head.

"We're not finished yet," Barbie huffed. She wiped her sweaty brow with the back of her hand. Up ahead the mountain loomed dark and dangerous.

Once again, Barbie glanced at the sky. It was now midmorning. "Come on! There's no time to lose."

Chapter Four

Barbie and Skylar continued hiking up Midnight Mountain toward the wizard's cave. The higher they went, the darker and colder it became.

The two hadn't gotten very far when Skylar whispered, "Do you see what I see?"

Barbie strained to see. In the distance, she thought she saw a large group of shiny black rocks. But could it be? Were the rocks moving?

"What is it?" Barbie asked. But even as she spoke the words, she realized the "rocks" were really hundreds of black crows. In one motion, all the birds flew into the air. The midmorning sky became dark, as if night had fallen instantly.

"Caw! Caw!" the large birds shrieked. Their cries filled the air.

Just then the birds began to dive at Barbie.

"Yikes!" she cried, raising her arms to cover her head. Skylar pressed close against Barbie's neck. Another crow flew right in front of her face. Then another, and another.

Barbie tried to run, but the air was filled with hundreds of screaming crows. Everywhere she turned, birds flew in circles around her. The noise they made was loud and sharp. Barbie covered her ears. At last she dropped to the ground and covered her head with her arms. The birds continued to circle overhead.

Then Barbie noticed something. The ground was covered with thousands of shiny black feathers. They had fallen from the crows' flapping wings. Barbie stayed low and began to gather the feathers. She emptied her cape and satchel of most of the leftover grass and pine needles. Then she stuffed handful after handful of black feathers into her satchel. Soon it was bulging with feathers.

Barbie took the satchel and swung it in the air over her head. This startled the birds, and they scattered. Before the birds returned, Barbie raced back down the path to the top of the waterfall.

Barbie could hear the crows behind her. "They must think they've frightened us off," she told Skylar. "Well, they're in for a big surprise."

"They are?" cried Skylar as they continued down the mountain. "You mean we're going back up there?"

"Yes, we are. This is the wizard's second obstacle," Barbie explained.

Soon they reached the burning rocks. Barbie sat down next to them. She took off her cape and ripped it in two. Then she spread it out on the ground. Skylar watched as she dumped the crows' feathers out of her satchel. Then she reached into the front pocket of her satchel and pulled out a few of her candles.

"Barbie, what are you doing? This is no time for arts and crafts!" Skylar shouted.

"Don't worry. You gave me an idea, Skylar," Barbie told him.

"I did? I mean, I did!" said the confused bird. Skylar watched as Barbie held the candles next to one of the burning rocks. The heat of the rock melted the candle wax. Quickly she dripped the wax onto the back of her cape.

While the wax was still soft and warm,

Barbie grabbed some feathers and began to press them into the wax. Row after row of shiny black feathers soon covered the back of the cape. When the wax cooled, the feathers were stuck.

"You did say I needed wings, didn't you?" Barbie reminded Skylar. The cape now looked like a huge pair of crow's wings.

Barbie swung the cape off the ground and draped it over her shoulders. She pulled the hood up over her head and went back up the path.

"It's a good idea. But you make a pretty weird-looking bird," Skylar observed.

"Well, let's hope those crows think so, too," Barbie said. The sound of the crows had just reached her ears. Soon she could see them.

Then, with a loud shriek of her own, Barbie raised her arms and rushed into the mass of crows. "Caw! Caw! Caw!" she cried, flapping her giant wings. "Leave us alone!" she shouted.

The birds had never seen anything like this

before! They all wanted to get away from the horrible giant crow. With a cry of fear, the crows flew off the mountain. They looked like a big, black cloud disappearing over the horizon.

As Barbie watched the crows disappear, she sat down to catch her breath. "Two obstacles down, one to go," she said, taking off her "wings."

Skylar looked at her and nodded. "I take it back, Barbie. You'd make a pretty good bird!"

Barbie smiled. "Well, thanks, Skylar. That's truly a compliment, coming from you."

Then Skylar added, "But crows aren't exactly the smartest birds in the nest, if you know what I mean."

Barbie laughed. The sun was high in the sky. It told her it was already noon. "Let's keep going. The wizard has only one more trap for us. And I want to know what it is."

Skylar whimpered, "I don't. Why don't you send me a postcard?"

Chapter Five

Barbie slowly made her way farther up the mountain. Her friend Skylar stayed on her shoulder to keep warm. Even though her magical daisy necklace protected her from the cold, Barbie's legs were beginning to ache.

Suddenly she stopped. "Oh, no!" she cried.

A deep, wide crack in the side of the mountain lay before her. She was cut off from the top of the mountain by this **chasm.** There was no way across it. She could begin to see flashes of lightning on the other side.

"Oh, Skylar," Barbie sighed, "I need wings

again! This must be the third obstacle!" She plopped down on a round, bumpy rock.

"Owww!" screamed a voice from underneath her. "How dare you!"

Barbie quickly scrambled back to her feet. The rock moved!

"Oh, please forgive me!" Barbie cried, looking around her. "I had no idea . . ."

But it wasn't a rock at all. It was a small, lumpy, brown troll. He had a large, hairy nose and three eyes. He **waddled** across the dirt and stared up at Barbie.

"Who are you?" the troll asked in a deep voice. "What are you doing here?"

"My name is Barbie," she replied. "And I'm trying to figure out how to cross this chasm."

The troll chuckled. "Oh, that's easy." The creature waved his twisted hand. A narrow bridge appeared across the chasm.

"Oh, thank you!" Barbie exclaimed,

stepping forward to cross.

"Not so fast, not so fast," the troll said, stepping in front of her. "You must pay to cross the bridge."

"Pay?" Barbie repeated in surprise. "But I have no money."

Suddenly the bridge disappeared. The troll's face twisted in anger.

"Then you'll never get across! I would never let someone like you cross my bridge, anyway," shouted the troll. He stamped his hairy foot. "You're too big! You talk too much! You don't have enough eyes! *And* you sat on me!"

The rude troll angered Skylar. The bluebird flew off Barbie's shoulder. "Stop saying those things!" the bird demanded. "She's my friend. And she must cross this bridge!"

Skylar flew into the face of the troll. But the troll simply reached out and grabbed the little bird.

"Be still," commanded the troll. "I could use a friend myself. Of course, I will have to cut out your tongue to keep you quiet."

"Let me go!" Skylar shouted angrily. Fear filled his eyes, and he looked at Barbie. "Help me!" he pleaded.

But Barbie simply looked at the troll and said, "You can have him, if you want. I agree that he talks too much. And his tongue would only grow back. But I have a better friend in my satchel."

"Some friend you are!" Skylar screeched at Barbie. But she didn't respond.

The troll was curious. "A better friend? What kind of friend do you have in there?"

"A very special one," Barbie explained. "He has bumpy brown skin and a dozen eyes. And I promise he won't say a word."

The troll glared at Barbie suspiciously. Then he said, "Your friend probably wouldn't like living here in the dirt and rocks."

Barbie replied, "Oh, yes, he would! Much more than that noisy bird. After I cross the bridge, I will give you my other friend."

The troll thought about Barbie's offer. He warned, "If you're tricking me—"

Barbie held up her hand. "I promise, no tricks! I will give you the friend in my sack for the friend you have in your hand. Shall we go?"

The troll nodded and let go of the bluebird. Skylar quickly flew to Barbie's shoulder. "Noisy? Well, I never," he began to say. But Barbie quickly silenced him.

The troll waved his arm toward the chasm. The bridge reappeared. Barbie swung her bag onto her shoulder and made her way across. The troll followed close behind, watching Barbie closely for any trick. The chasm was deep, and the bridge shook and trembled. Lightning cut through the sky as the wind howled beneath her.

At last she was safely across.

"Well," yelled the troll, "where's my friend?"

Barbie smiled sweetly at the troll. "Right here," she said. She reached into her bag and felt around. When she pulled out her hand, she was holding a big, lumpy, dirty potato. She tossed it to him.

The troll caught the potato and examined it closely. "Why, he's beautiful," he whispered. He pointed to the small dents in the skin. "Look how many lovely 'eyes' he has. And he hasn't made a sound. You were right. He's much nicer than a noisy bird."

Barbie grinned. The rude, angry troll was changed into a happy, smiling little fellow.

"He will be a loyal friend. And I'm sure you'll take very

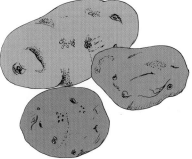

good care of him," Barbie said kindly.

The troll nodded and wandered off. He was cradling the potato in his hands, humming a gentle tune.

"Whew, that was a close call," Skylar sighed in relief. "I've never been so scared in my life."

"I hope you know I would never let that troll harm you," Barbie told her friend. Skylar gently rubbed his head against her cheek.

Then Barbie glanced worriedly at the sky. It was early afternoon. They pushed on. It was very cold now. Patches of ice and snow dotted the rocky path. Before long they reached the top of Midnight Mountain.

"There it is," said Barbie **anxiously.** "The wizard's cave."

Chapter Six

Barbie and Skylar could see light coming from inside the cave. Smoke puffed out of the opening. Barbie tiptoed closer. She sniffed and wrinkled her nose. "What a terrible smell! The poor unicorn must be miserable. Let's go."

"Do we have to, Barbie?" Skylar asked, hiding behind her. "I'm just a little bird. I'm no match for a wizard. He'll turn me into a worm!"

"We can do it together," Barbie declared.

"I can't. I'm too scared," Skylar admitted. "I want to go home." The bird began to flutter his wings. Barbie tried to calm him down. But it was no use. In a panic, Skylar flew away.

"Wait!" Barbie cried. But Skylar didn't return. Now Barbie was all alone. "I've come too far to give up now," she thought. She crept to the entrance of the cave and peeked around the corner.

The cave was lit by a fire burning in the center area. A large black kettle sat bubbling on the fire. The walls **oozed** with bright-green slime.

There were shelves everywhere covered with jars.

Then Barbie caught sight of the wizard. He was dressed in a long, purple robe. He was tall, with a crooked nose and wild, white hair. The unicorn was tied to a post behind him.

The wizard went to the kettle and dropped

42

something in it. He took a deep breath and smiled. Barbie caught a whiff and almost got sick.

The wizard laughed wickedly and rubbed his hands together. "Once you drink this," he said to the unicorn, "your power will be mine!"

The unicorn stomped and pulled hard at the ropes that held her.

"How am I ever going to get past the wizard?" thought Barbie.

Just then a deep, scratchy voice called out, "Come in! Come in! I've been expecting you."

Trembling, Barbie stepped into the cave. Her hand went up to the flower chain around her neck. "Was the Queen of the Fairies right? Will this really protect me?" she wondered.

"I must thank you," the wizard said, "for breaking the spell of the Enchanted Glade. You helped me capture the unicorn."

Barbie's face burned with anger. She stepped toward the wizard and commanded, "Let her go!"

a shiver run down her spine.

The wizard continued, "I see that the talking bird has left you. You are only a human. Why should you care about the forest when its creatures don't care about you? So is it a deal?"

Barbie stared at the wizard. "I guess I have no choice," she said slowly. Barbie turned to leave. Then she heard the wizard call out, "And take off that horrible necklace. The smell sickens me."

Barbie's shoulders slumped as she walked out of the cave. With deep sorrow in her heart, Barbie ran down the mountain. What was she going to do? She couldn't betray the Queen of the Fairies. But she couldn't let her village freeze, either. She stopped to catch her breath. Then she sank to the ground and buried her head in her hands.

Suddenly she felt soft feathers brush against her cheek. "Barbie! It's me."

"Skylar," Barbie said quietly.

"I'm so glad you're okay," the bird chirped.

"I'm so sorry I left you. I won't do it again, I promise. I'll even go back to the wizard's cave with you! That is, if you still need me."

Barbie gazed at her friend and smiled. "Of course I need you, you birdbrain," she laughed. Then she told him about the wizard's offer.

"Barbie, you can't betray the Queen of the Fairies! You wouldn't!" Skylar cried.

"Of course not. But I have to do *something.*" She thought for a moment. Then she brightened. "Did you mean what you said? Will you really go back with me to the wizard's cave?"

"Yes, you have my word," Skylar replied seriously. "But how can we free the unicorn?"

"Don't worry," Barbie said. "I have an idea."

Skylar groaned, "Oh, no, here we go again!"

Barbie grabbed her satchel and dumped out what was left in it: some grass, a few feathers, some bread and raspberries, a candle, and a lantern. Barbie carefully removed the four pieces of glass in the lantern. Then she quickly crushed the berries until they made red juice. Barbie dripped the juice onto the glass. Instantly, the brightly colored juice froze onto the glass.

Skylar shivered. "Barbie, this is no time to be making ice pops," he protested. "It's getting colder. Time must be running out!"

"I know," said Barbie. "Hold on!" Then she carefully replaced the four sides of her lantern. When she held the lantern up to the fading sunshine, it glowed with a pink light.

She took off the daisy necklace and put it in her sack. She grabbed the candle, some sharp rocks, and some dead grass. "Let's go, Skylar. I'll explain the rest of my plan on the way."

The friends approached the wizard's cave again. There wasn't much time. Quickly Barbie started a small fire by rubbing the rocks together next to the grass. Before the fire burned out, she used it to light the candle in the lantern. As Barbie entered the cave, she held the lantern by her side. The wizard was by the kettle. His back was to her.

"I have something for you," Barbie called.

The wizard spun around. He glared at her. "You have captured the Queen of the Fairies? I don't believe you," he cackled.

"See for yourself," Barbie said, holding the lantern up in front of her. Rose-colored, sparkling light flickered on the walls. The wizard rushed over to Barbie. "Give her to me!" he shouted and **seized** the lantern from Barbie's hands. He flung open the lantern's tiny door to grab the queen. Instead, the candle's hot flame burned his hand.

"Aaah!" the wizard shrieked. "How dare you trick me. You'll pay for this, you fool!"

"*Now, Skylar!*" Barbie commanded. The

bluebird flew out of Barbie's satchel. The daisy necklace was in his beak. In one swift motion, Skylar dropped it around the wizard's neck.

"Aaah!" the wizard screamed again. "Those cursed—!" But the wizard never finished. He had turned into a puddle of green slime on the floor.

Skylar swooped over the puddle and then landed on Barbie's shoulder. "Yuck! That smells awful. Barbie, how did you know the flowers would make the wizard melt?"

"I didn't," Barbie sighed with relief. "But I knew the wizard was afraid of my necklace. The queen said it was magical. I was just hoping it would give us enough time to free the unicorn."

"Speaking of time," Skylar pointed out, "we'd better hurry. It's almost sundown! We still have to get the unicorn to the Enchanted Glade."

Barbie quickly untied the ropes. The unicorn shook her head and whinnied in happiness.

"Let's go!" Barbie called, hopping onto the

unicorn's back. Taking one last look at the empty cave, she could see the dark, dreary place begin to brighten. And all three friends knew that the wizard would never harm anyone again.

Though it had taken Barbie hours to climb up, the three made it down the mountain in no time. The wizard's traps had disappeared, just like the wizard himself.

They reached the Enchanted Glade not a moment too soon. A warm ray of sunshine fell on everything. Instantly, the trees became green again. Flowers sprang from the earth. The waterfall gurgled as it flowed down the side of the mountain. The Enchanted Glade had been saved!

Barbie leaned over and gave the unicorn a hug. "I'm glad you're okay," she told the noble animal. Then she looked at Skylar, who flew over to her shoulder. "And you were very brave."

"You both were," sang a soft, sweet voice. "Thank you."

Barbie could see a rose-colored light in one of the trees. It was the Queen of the Fairies. Barbie bowed her head. "You're welcome. I promise I will never disturb this glade again."

The fairy queen fluttered over to Skylar and kissed him on the top of his head. The forest lit up with hundreds of tiny, sparkly lights as the other fairies flew throughout the kingdom to celebrate.

For once, Skylar was speechless.

Barbie laughed. "Well, Skylar, it's time for me to go home to my cottage."

The bluebird flew up into the air. "I'll lead the way. But I was thinking, since the queen was so pleased, maybe you and I could continue our fight against evil. There's a dragon on the other side of Midnight Mountain. Maybe we could—"

Barbie gently pinched the little bird's beak closed to silence him. "Oh, no, my fine feathered friend," Barbie told him. "I have had enough adventure for quite a while!"